MY UNCLE IS THE COOLEST

BECAUSE . . . .

4

HOME 48

9

HE LOVES TO TAKE ME FOR A DRIVE IN HIS COOL CAR

13

HE LETS ME WIN WHEN
WE PLAY BASKETBALL

14

15

HE ALWAYS REMEMBERS
MY BIRTHDAY

16

THANK YOU UNCLE

............THE END

Made in the USA
Middletown, DE
14 December 2019